THE LION OF TIBERIAS

BY

ROBERT E. HOWARD

British Library Cataloguing-in-Publication Data
A catalogue record for this book is available from the
British Library

Contents

Robert E. Howard

Robert Ervin Howard was born in Peaster, Texas in 1906. During his youth, his family moved between a variety of Texan boomtowns, and Howard – a bookish and somewhat introverted child – was steeped in the violent myths and legends of the Old South. Although he loved reading and learning, Howard developed a distinctly Texan, hardboiled outlook on the world. He became a passionate fan of boxing, taking it up at an amateur level, and from the age of nine began to write adventure tales of semi-historical bloodshed. In 1919, when Howard was thirteen, his family moved to the Central Texas hamlet of Cross Plains, where he would stay for the rest of his life.

At fifteen Howard began to read the pulp magazines of the day, and to write more seriously. The December 1922 issue of his high school newspaper featured two of his stories, 'Golden Hope Christmas' and 'West is West'. In 1924 he sold his first piece – a short caveman tale titled 'Spear and Fang' – for $16 to the not-yet-famous *Weird Tales* magazine. He published with the magazine regularly over the next few years. 1929 was a breakout year for Howard, in that the 23-year-old writer began to sell to other magazines, such as *Ghost Stories* and *Argosy*, both of whom had previously sent him hundreds of rejection slips. In 1930, he began a correspondence with weird fiction master H. P. Lovecraft which ran up to his death six years later, and is regarded as one of the great correspondence cycles in all of fantasy literature.

It was partly due to Lovecraft's encouragement that Howard created his most famous character, Conan the Cimmerian. Conan – a barbarian-turned-King during the Hyborian Age, a mythical period of some 12,000 years ago – featured in seventeen *Weird Tales* stories between 1933 and 1936, and is now regarded as having spawned the 'sword and sorcery' genre, making Howard's influence on fantasy literature comparable to that of J. R. R. Tolkien's. The Conan stories have since been adapted many times, most famously in the series of films starring Arnold Schwarzenegger.

Howard was enjoying an all-time high in sales by the beginning of 1936, but he was also deeply upset by the ill health of his mother, who had fallen into a coma. On the morning of June 11, 1936, he asked an attending nurse whether she would ever recover, and the nurse replied negatively. Howard walked to his car, parked outside the family home in Cross Plains, and shot himself. He died eight hours later, aged just thirty.

CHAPTER 1

The battle in the meadowlands of the Euphrates was over, but not the slaughter. On that bloody field where the Caliph of Bagdad and his Turkish allies had broken the onrushing power of Doubeys ibn Sadaka of Hilla and the desert, the steel-clad bodies lay strewn like the drift of a storm. The great canal men called the Nile, which connected the Euphrates with the distant Tigris, was choked with the bodies of the tribesmen, and survivors were panting in flight toward the white walls of Hilla which shimmered in the distance above the placid waters of the nearer river. Behind them the mailed hawks, the Seljuks, rode down the fleeing, cutting the fugitives from their saddles. The glittering dream of the Arab emir had ended in a storm of blood and steel, and his spurs struck blood as he rode for the distant river.

Yet at one spot in the littered field the fight still swirled and eddied, where the emir's favorite son, Achmet, a slender lad of seventeen or eighteen, stood at bay with one companion. The mailed riders swooped in, struck and reined back, yelling in baffled rage before the lashing of the great sword in this man's hands. His was a figure alien and incongruous, his red mane contrasting with the black locks about him no less than his dusty gray mail contrasted with the plumed burnished headpieces and silvered hauberks of

3

the slayers. He was tall and powerful, with a wolfish hardness of limbs and frame that his mail could not conceal. His dark, scarred face was moody, his blue eyes cold and hard as the blue steel whereof Rhineland gnomes forge swords for heroes in northern forests.

Little of softness had there been in John Norwald's life. Son of a house ruined by the Norman conquest, this descendant of feudal thanes had only memories of wattle-thatched huts and the hard life of a man-at-arms, serving for poor hire barons he hated. Born in north England, the ancient Danelagh, long settled by blue-eyed vikings, his blood was neither Saxon nor Norman, but Danish, and the grim unbreakable strength of the blue North was his. From each stroke of life that felled him, he rose fiercer and more unrelenting. He had not found existence easier in his long drift East which led him into the service of Sir William de Montserrat, seneschal of a castle on the frontier beyond Jordan.

In all his thirty years, John Norwald remembered but one kindly act, one deed of mercy; wherefore he now faced a whole host, desperate fury nerving his iron arms.

It had been Achmet's first raid, whereby his riders had trapped de Montserrat and a handful of retainers. The boy had not shrunk from the swordplay, but the savagery that butchers fallen foes was not his. Writhing in the bloody dust, stunned and half-dead, John Norwald had dimly seen the lifted scimitar thrust aside by a slender arm, and the face of the youth bending above him, the dark eyes filled with tears of pity.

Too gentle for the age and his manner of life, Achmet had made his astounded warriors take up the wounded Frank and bring him with them. And in the weeks that passed while Norwald's wounds healed, he lay in Achmet's tent by an oasis of the Asad tribes, tended by the lad's own hakim. When he could ride again, Achmet had brought him to Hilla. Doubeys ibn Sadaka always tried to humor his son's whims, and now, though muttering pious horror in his beard, he granted Norwald his life. Nor did he regret it, for in the grim Englishman he found a fighting-man worth any three of his own hawks.

John Norwald felt no tugging of loyalty toward de Montserrat, who had fled out of the ambush leaving him in the hands of the Moslems, nor toward the race at whose hands he had had only hard knocks all his life. Among the Arabs he found an environment congenial to his moody, ferocious nature, and he plunged into the turmoil of desert feuds, forays and border wars as if he had been born under a Bedouin black felt tent instead of a Yorkshire thatch. Now, with the failure of ibn Sadaka's thrust at Bagdad and sovereignty, the Englishman found himself once more hemmed in by chanting foes, mad with the tang of blood. About him and his youthful comrade swirled the wild riders of Mosul; the mailed hawks of Wasit and Bassorah, whose lord, Zenghi Imad ed din, had that day out-maneuvered ibn Sadaka and slashed his shining host to pieces.

On foot among the bodies of their warriors, their backs to a wall of dead horses and men, Achmet and John Norwald beat back the onslaught. A heron-feathered emir reined in his Turkoman steed, yelling his war-cry, his house-troops swirling in behind him.

"Back, boy; leave him to me!" grunted the Englishman, thrusting Achmet behind him. The slashing scimitar struck blue sparks from his basinet and his great sword dashed the Seljuk dead from his saddle. Bestriding the chieftain's body, the giant Frank lashed up at the shrieking swordsmen who spurred in, leaning from their saddles to swing their blades. The curved sabers shivered on his shield and armor, and his long sword crashed through bucklers, breastplates, and helmets, cleaving flesh and splintering bones, littering corpses at his iron-sheathed feet. Panting and howling the survivors reined back.

Then a roaring voice made them glance quickly about, and they fell back as a tall, strongly built horseman rode through them and drew rein before the grim Frank and his slender companion. John Norwald for the first time stood face to face with Zenghi esh Shami, Imad ed din, governor of Wasit and warden of Basorah, whom men called the Lion of Tiberias, because of his exploits at the siege of Tiberias.

The Englishman noted the breadth of the mighty steel-clad shoulders, the grip of the powerful hands on rein and sword-hilt; the blazing magnetic blue eyes, setting off the ruthless lines of the dark face. Under the thin black lines of the mustaches the wide lips smiled, but it was the merciless grin of the hunting panther.

Zenghi spoke and there was at the back of his powerful voice a hint of mockery or gargantuan mirth that rose above wrath and slaughter.

"Who are these paladins that they stand among their prey like tigers in their den, and none is found to go against them? Is it Rustem whose heel is on the necks of my emirs--or only a renegade Nazarene? And the other, by Allah, unless I am mad, it is the cub of the desert wolf! Are you not Achmet ibn Doubeys?"

It was Achmet who answered; for Norwald maintained a grim silence, watching the Turk through slit eyes, fingers locked on his bloody hilt.

"It is so, Zenghi esh Shami," answered the youth proudly, "and this is my brother at arms, John Norwald. Bid your wolves ride on, oh prince. Many of them have fallen. More shall fall before their steel tastes our hearts."

Zenghi shrugged his mighty shoulders, in the grip of the mocking devil that lurks at the heart of all the sons of high Asia.

"Lay down your weapons, wolf-cub and Frank. I swear by the honor of my clan, no sword shall touch you."

"I trust him not," growled John Norwald. "Let him come a pace nearer and I'll take him to Hell with us."

"Nay," answered Achmet. "The prince keeps his word. Lay down your sword, my brother. We have done all men might do. My father the emir will ransom us."

He tossed down his scimitar with a boyish sigh of unashamed relief, and Norwald grudgingly laid down his broadsword.

"I had rather sheathe it in his body," he growled.

Achmet turned to the conqueror and spread his hands.

"Oh, Zenghi--" he began, when the Turk made a quick gesture, and the two prisoners found themselves seized and their hands bound behind them with thongs that cut the flesh.

"There is no need of that, prince," protested Achmet. "We have given ourselves into your hands. Bid your men loose us. We will not seek to escape."

"Be silent, cub!" snapped Zenghi. The Turk's eyes still danced with dangerous laughter, but his face was dark with passion. He reined nearer. "No sword shall touch you, young dog," he said deliberately. "Such was my word, and I keep my oaths. No blade shall come near you, yet the vultures shall pluck your bones tonight. Your dog-sire escaped me, but you shall not escape, and when men tell him of your end, he will tear his locks in anguish."

Achmet, held in the grip of the powerful soldiers, looked up, paling, but answered without a quaver of fear.

"Are you then a breaker of oaths, Turk?"

"I break no oath," answered the lord of Wasit. "A whip is not a sword."

His hand came up, gripping a terrible Turkoman scourge, to the seven rawhide thongs of which bits of lead were fastened. Leaning from his saddle as he struck, he brought those metal-weighted thongs down across the boy's face with terrible force. Blood spurted and one of Achmet's eyes was half torn from its socket. Held helpless, the boy could not evade the blows Zenghi rained upon him. But not a whimper escaped him, though his features turned to a bloody, raw, ghastly and eyeless ruin beneath the ripping strokes that shredded the flesh and splintered the bones beneath. Only at last a low animal-like moaning drooled from his mangled lips as he hung senseless and dying in the hands of his captors.

Without a cry or a word John Norwald watched, while the heart in his breast shriveled and froze and turned to ice that naught could touch or thaw or break. Something died in his soul and in its place rose an elemental spirit unquenchable as frozen fire and bitter as hoarfrost.

The deed was done. The mangled broken horror that had been Prince Achmet iby Doubeys was cast carelessly on a heap of dead, a touch of life still pulsing through the tortured limbs. On the crimson mask of his features fell the shadow of vulture wings in the sunset. Zenghi threw aside the dripping scourge and turned to the silent Frank. But when he met the burning eyes of his captive, the smile faded from the prince's lips and the taunts died unspoken. In those cold, terrible eyes the Turk read hate beyond common conception--a monstrous, burning, almost tangible thing, drawn up from the lower pits of Hell, not to be dimmed by time or suffering.

The Turk shivered as from a cold unseen wind. Then he regained his composure. "I give you life, infidel," said Zenghi, "because of my oath. You have seen something of my power. Remember it in the long dreary years when you shall regret my mercy, and howl for death. And know that as I serve you, I will serve all Christendom. I have come into Outremer and left their castles desolate; I have ridden eastward with the heads of their chiefs swinging at my saddle. I will come again, not as a raider but as a conqueror. I will sweep their hosts into the sea. Frankistan shall howl for her dead kings, and my horses shall stamp in the citadels of the infidel; for on this field I set my feet on the glittering stairs that lead to empire."

"This is my only word to you, Zenghi, dog of Tiberias," answered the Frank in a voice he did not himself recognize. "In a year, or ten years, or twenty years, I will come again to you, to pay this debt."

"Thus spake the trapped wolf to the hunter," answered Zenghi, and turning to the memluks who held Norwald, he said, "Place him among the unransomed captives. Take him to Bassorah and see that he is sold as a galley-slave. He is strong and may live for four or five years."

The sun was setting in crimson, gloomy and sinister for the fugitives who staggered toward the distant towers of Hilla that the setting sun tinted in blood. But the land was as one flooded with the scarlet glory of imperial pageantry to the Caliph who stood on a hillock, lifting his voice to Allah who had once more vindicated the dominance of his chosen viceroy, and saved the sacred City of Peace from violation.

"Verily, verily, a young lion has risen in Islam, to be as a sword and shield to the Faithful, to revive the power of Muhammad, and to confound the infidels!"

CHAPTER 2

Prince Zenghi was the son of a slave, which was no great handicap in that day, when the Seljuk emperors, like the Ottomans after them, ruled through slave generals and satraps. His father, Ak Sunkur, had held high posts under the sultan Melik Shah, and as a young boy Zenghi had been taken under the special guidance of that war-hawk Kerbogha of Mosul. The young eagle was not a Seljuk; his sires were Turks from beyond the Oxus, of that people which men later called Tatars. Men of this blood were rapidly becoming the dominant factor in western Asia, as the empire of the Seljuks, who had enslaved and trained them in the art of ruling, began to crumble. Emirs were stirring restlessly under the relaxing yoke of the sultans. The Seljuks were reaping the yield of the seeds of the feudal system they had sown, and among the jealous sons of Melik Shah there was none strong enough to rebuild the crumbling lines.

So far the fiefs, held by feudal vassals of the sultans, were at least nominally loyal to the royal masters, but already there was beginning the slow swirling upheaval that ultimately reared kingdoms on the ruins of the old empire. The driving impetus of one man advanced this movement more than anything else--the vital dynamic power of Zenghi esh Shami--Zenghi the Syrian, so called because of his exploits against the Crusaders in Syria. Popular legendry has passed him by, to exalt Saladin who followed and overshadowed him; yet he was the forerunner of the great Moslem heroes who were to shatter the Crusading kingdoms, and but for him the shining deeds of Saladin might never have come to pass.

In the dim and misty pageantry of phantoms that move shadow-like through those crimson years, one figure stands out clear and bold-etched--a figure on a rearing black stallion, the black silken cloak flowing from his mailed shoulders, the dripping scimitar in his hand. He is Zenghi, son of the pagan nomads, the first of a glittering line of magnificent conquerors before whom the iron men of Christendom reeled--Nur-ad-din, Saladin, Baibars, Kalawun, Bayazid--aye, and Subotai, Genghis Khan, Hulagu, Tamerlane, and Suleiman the Great.

In 1124 the fall of Tyre to the Crusaders marked the high tide of Frankish power in Asia. Thereafter the hammer-strokes of Islam fell on a waning sovereignty. At the time of the battle of the Euphrates the kingdom of Outremer extended from Edessa in the north to Ascalon in the south, a distance of some five hundred miles. Yet it was in few places more than fifty miles broad, from east to west, and walled Moslem towns were within a day's ride of Christian keeps. Such a condition could not exist forever. That it existed as long as it did was owing partly to the indomitable valor of the cross-wearers, and partly to the lack of a strong leader among the Moslems.

In Zenghi such a leader was found. When he broke ibn Sadaka he was thirty-eight years of age, and had held his fief of Wasit but a year. Thirty-six was the minimum age at which the sultans allowed a man to hold a governorship, and most notables were much older when they were so honored than was Zenghi. But the honor only whetted his ambition.

The same sun that shone mercilessly on John Norwald, stumbling along in chains on the road that led to the galley's bench, gleamed on Zenghi's gilded mail as he rode north to enter the service of the sultan Muhammad at Hamadhan. His boast that his feet were set on the stairs of fame was no idle one. All orthodox Islam vied in honoring him.

To the Franks who had felt his talons in Syria, came faint tidings of that battle beside the Nile canal, and they heard other word of his growing power. There came tidings of a dispute between sultan and Caliph, and of Zenghi turning against his former master, riding into Bagdad with the banners of Muhammad. Honors rained like stars on his turban, sang the Arab minstrels. Warden of Bagdad, governor of Irak, prince of el Jezira, Atabeg of Mosul--on up the glittering stairs of power rode Zenghi, while the Franks ignored the tidings from the East with the perverse blindness of their race--until Hell burst along their borders and the roar of the Lion shook their towers.

Outposts and castles went up in flames, and Christian throats felt the knife edge, Christian necks the yoke of slavery. Outside the walls of doomed Athalib, Baldwin, king of Jerusalem, saw his picked chivalry swept broken and flying into the desert. Again at Barin the Lion drove Baldwin and his Damascene allies headlong in flight, and when the Emperor of Byzantium himself, John Comnene, moved against the victorious Turk, he found himself chasing a desert wind that turned unexpectedly and slaughtered his stragglers, and harried his lines until life was a burden and a stone about his royal neck. John Comnene decided that his Moslem neighbors were no more to be despised than his barbaric Frankish allies, and before he sailed away from the Syrian coast he held secret parleys with Zenghi that bore crimson fruit in later years. His going left the Turk free to move against his eternal enemies, the Franks. His objective was Edessa, northernmost stronghold of the Christians, and one of the most powerful of their cities. But like a crafty swordsman he blinded his foes by feints and gestures.

Outremer reeled before his blows. The land was filled with the chanting of the riders, the twang of bows, and the whine of swords. Zenghi's hawks swept through the land and their horses hoofs spattered blood on the standards of kings. Walled castles toppled in flame, sword-hacked corpses strewed the valleys, dark hands knotted in the yellow tresses of screaming women, and the lords of the Franks cried out in wrath and pain. Up the glittering stairs of empire rode Zenghi on his black stallion, his scimitar dripping in his hand, stars jeweling his turban.

And while he swept the land like a storm, and hurled down barons to make drinking-cups of their skulls and stables of their palaces, the galley-slaves, whispering to one another in their eternal darkness where the oars clacked everlastingly and the lap of the waves was a symphony of slow madness, spoke of a red-haired giant who never spoke, and whom neither labor, nor starvation, nor the dripping lash, nor the drag of the bitter years could break.

The years passed, glittering, star-strewn, gilt-spangled years to the rider in the shining saddle, to the lord in the golden-domed palace; black, silent, bitter years in the creaking, reeking, rat-haunted darkness of the galleys.

CHAPTER 3

"He rides on the wind with the stars in his hair;
Like Death falls his shadow on castles and towns;
And the kings of the Caphars cry out in despair.
For the hoofs of his stallion have trampled their
crowns."

Thus sang a wandering Arab minstrel in the tavern of
a little outpost village which stood on the ancient--and now
little-traveled--road from Antioch to Aleppo. The village was
a cluster of mud huts huddling about a castle-crowned hill.
The population was mongrel--Syrians, Arabs, mixed breeds
with Frankish blood in their veins.

Tonight a representative group was gathered in the inn-
-native laborers from the fields; a lean Arab herdsman or two;
French men-at-arms in worn leather and rusty mail, from the
castle on the hill; a pilgrim wandered off his route to the holy
places of the south; the ragged minstrel. Two figures held the
attention of casual lookers-on. They sat on opposite sides of
a rudely carved table, eating meat and drinking wine, and
they were evidently strangers to each other, since no word
passed between them, though each glanced surreptitiously at
the other from time to time.

Both were tall, hard limbed and broad shouldered, but there the resemblance ended. One was clean-shaven, with a hawk-like predatory face from which keen blue eyes gleamed coldly. His burnished helmet lay on the bench beside him with the kite-shaped shield, and his mail coif was pushed back, revealing a mass of red-gold hair. His armor gleamed with gilt-work and silver chasing, and the hilt of his broadsword sparkled with jewels.

The man opposite him seemed drab by comparison, with his dusty gray chain mail and worn sword-hilt untouched by any gleam of gem or gold. His square-cut tawny mane was matched by a short beard which masked the strong lines of jaw and chin.

The minstrel finished his song with an exultant clash of the strings, and eyed his audience half in insolence, half in uneasiness.

"And thus, masters," he intoned, one eye on possible alms, the other on the door. "Zenghi, prince of Wasit, brought his memluks up the Tigris on boats to aid the sultan Muhammad who lay encamped about the walls of Bagdad. Then, when the Caliph saw the banners of Zenghi, he said, 'Lo, now is come up against me the young lion who overthrew ibn Sadaka for me; open the gates, friends, and throw yourselves on his mercy, for there is none found to stand before him.' And it was done, and the sultan gave to Zenghi all the land of el Jezira.

"Gold and power flowed through his fingers. Mosul, his capital, which he found a waste of ruins, he made to bloom as roses blossom by an oasis. Kings trembled before him but the poor rejoiced, for he shielded them from the sword. His servants looked on him as upon God. Of him it is told that he gave a slave a husk to hold, and not for a year did he ask for it. Then when he demanded it, lo, the man gave it into his hands, wrapped in a napkin, and for his diligence Zenghi gave him command of a castle. For though the Atabeg is a hard master, yet he is just to True Believers."

The knight in the gleaming mail flung the minstrel a coin.

"Well sung, pagan!" he cried in a harsh voice that sounded the Norman-French words strangely. "Know you the song of the sack of Edessa?"

"Aye, my lord," smirked the minstrel, "and with the favor of your lordships I will essay it."

"Your head shall roll on the floor first," spoke the other knight suddenly in a voice deep and somber with menace. "It is enough that you praise the dog Zenghi in our teeth. No man sings of his butcheries at Edessa, beneath a Christian roof in my presence."

The minstrel blenched and gave back, for the cold gray eyes of the Frank were grim. The knight in the ornate mail looked at the speaker curiously, no resentment in his reckless dancing eyes.

"You speak as one to whom the subject is a sore one, friend," said he.

The other fixed his somber stare on his questioner, but made no reply save a slight shrug of his mighty mailed shoulders as he continued his meal.

"Come," persisted the stranger, "I meant no offense. I am newly come to these parts--I am Sir Roger d'Ibelin, vassal to the king of Jerusalem. I have fought Zenghi in the south, when Baldwin and Anar of Damascus made alliance against him, and I only wished to hear the details of the taking of Edessa. By God, there were few Christians who escaped to bear the tale."

"I crave pardon for my seeming discourtesy," returned the other. "I am Miles du Courcey, in the service of the prince of Antioch. I was in Edessa when it fell.

"Zenghi came up from Mosul and laid waste the Diyar Bekr, taking town after town from the Seljuks. Count Joscelin de Courtenay was dead, and the rule was in the hands of that sluggard, Joscelin II. In the late fall of the year Zenghi laid siege to Amid, and the count bestirred himself--but only to march away to Turbessel with all his household.

"We were left at Edessa with the town in charge of fat Armenian merchants who gripped their moneybags and trembled in fear of Zenghi, unable to overcome their swinish avarice enough to pay the mongrel mercenaries Joscelin had left to defend the city.

"Well, as anyone might know, Zenghi left Amid and marched against us as soon as word reached him that the poor fool Joscelin had departed. He reared his siege engines over against the walls, and day and night hurled assaults against the gates and towers, which had never fallen had we had the proper force to man them.

"But to give them their due, our wretched mercenaries did well. There was no rest or ease for any of us; day and night the ballistas creaked, stones and beams crashed against the towers, arrows blinded the sky in their whistling clouds, and Zenghi's chanting devils swarmed up the walls. We beat them back until our swords were broken, our mail hung in bloody tatters, and our arms were dead with weariness. For a month we kept Zenghi at bay, waiting for Count Joscelin, but he never came.

"It was on the morning of December 23rd that the rams and engines made a great breach in the outer wall, and the Moslems came through like a river bursting through a dam. The defenders died like flies along the broken ramparts, but human power could not stem that tide. The memluks rode into the streets and the battle became a massacre. The Turkish sword knew no mercy. Priests died at their altars, women in their courtyards, children at their play. Bodies choked the streets, the gutters ran crimson, and through it all rode Zenghi on his black stallion like a phantom of Death."

"Yet you escaped?"

The cold gray eyes became more somber.

"I had a small band of men-at-arms. When I was dashed senseless from my saddle by a Turkish mace, they took me up and rode for the western gate. Most of them died in the winding streets, but the survivors brought me to safety. When I recovered my senses the city lay far behind me.

"But I rode back." The speaker seemed to have forgotten his audience. His eyes were distant, withdrawn; his bearded chin rested on his mailed fist; he seemed to be speaking to himself. "Aye, I had ridden into the teeth of Hell itself. But I met a servant, fallen death-stricken among the straggling fugitives, and ere he died he told me that she whom I sought was dead--struck down by a memluk's scimitar."

Shaking his iron-clad shoulders he roused himself as from a bitter revelry. His eyes grew cold and hard again; the harsh timbre re-entered his voice.

"Two years have seen a great change in Edessa I hear. Zenghi rebuilt the walls and has made it one of his strongest holds. Our hold on the land is crumbling and tearing away. With a little aid, Zenghi will surge over Outremer and obliterate all vestiges of Christendom."

"That aid may come from the north," muttered a bearded man-at-arms. "I was in the train of the barons who marched with John Comnene when Zenghi outmaneuvered him. The emperor has no love for us."

"Bah! He is at least a Christian," laughed the man who called himself d'Ibelin, running his restless fingers through his clustering golden locks.

Du Courcey's cold eyes narrowed suddenly as they rested on a heavy golden ring of curious design on the other's finger, but he said nothing.

Heedless of the intensity of the Norman's stare, d'Ibelin rose and tossed a coin on the table to pay his reckoning. With a careless word of farewell to the idlers he rose and strode out of the inn with a clanking of armor. The men inside heard him shouting impatiently for his horse. And Sir Miles du Courcey rose, took up shield and helmet, and followed.

The man known as d'Ibelin had covered perhaps a half-mile, and the castle on the hill was but a faint bulk behind him, gemmed by a few points of light, when a drum of hoofs made him wheel with a guttural oath that was not French. In the dim starlight he made out the form of his recent inn companion, and he laid hand on his jeweled hilt. Du Courcey drew up beside him and spoke to the grimly silent figure.

"Antioch lies the other way, good sir. Perhaps you have taken the wrong road by mischance. Three hours' ride in this direction will bring you into Saracen territory."

"Friend," retorted the other, "I have not asked your advice concerning my road. Whether I go east or west is scarcely your affair."

"As vassal to the prince of Antioch it is my affair to inquire into suspicious actions within his domain. When I see a man traveling under false pretenses, with a Saracen ring on his finger, riding by night toward the border, it seems suspicious enough for me to make inquiries."

"I can explain my actions if I see fit," bruskly answered d'Ibelin, "but these insulting accusations I will answer at the sword's point. What mean you by false pretensions?"

"You are not Roger d'Ibelin. You are not even a Frenchman."

"No?" a sneer rasped in the other's voice as he slipped his sword from its sheath.

"No. I have been to Constantinople, and seen the northern mercenaries who serve the Greek emperor. I can not forget your hawk face. You are John Comnene's spy--Wulfgar Edric's son, a captain in the Varangian Guard."

A wild beast snarl burst from the masquerader's lips and his horse screamed and leaped convulsively as he struck in the spurs, throwing all his frame behind his sword arm as the beast plunged. But du Courcey was too seasoned a fighter to be caught so easily. With a wrench of his rein he brought his steed round, rearing. The Varangian's frantic horse plunged past, and the whistling sword struck fire from the Norman's lifted shield. With a furious yell the fierce Norman wheeled again to the assault, and the horses reared together while the swords of their riders hissed, circled in flashing arcs, and fell with ringing clash on mail-links or shield.

The men fought in grim silence, save for the panting of straining effort, but the clangor of their swords awoke the still night and sparks flew as from a blacksmith's anvil. Then with a deafening crash a broadsword shattered a helmet and splintered the skull within. There followed a loud clash of armor as the loser fell heavily from his saddle. A riderless horse galloped away, and the conqueror, shaking the sweat from his eyes, dismounted and bent above the motionless steel-clad figure.

CHAPTER 4

On the road that leads south from Edessa to Rakka, the Moslem host lay encamped, the lines of gay-colored pavilions spread out in the plains. It was a leisurely march, with wagons, luxurious equipment, and whole households with women and slaves. After two years in Edessa the Atabeg of Mosul was returning to his capital by the way of Rakka. Fires glimmered in the gathering dusk where the first stars were peeping; lutes twanged and voices were lifted in song and laughter about the cooking pots.

Before Zenghi, playing at chess with his friend and chronicler, the Arab Ousama of Sheyzar, came the eunuch Yaruktash, who salaamed low and in his squeaky voice intoned, "Oh, Lion of Islam, an emir of the infidels desires audience with thee--the captain of the Greeks who is called Wulfgar Edric's son. The chief Il-Ghazi and his memluks came upon him, riding alone, and would have slain him but he threw up his arm and on his hand they saw the ring thou gavest the emperor as a secret sign for his messengers."

Zenghi tugged his gray-shot black beard and grinned, well pleased.

"Let him be brought before me." The slave bowed and withdrew.

To Ousama, Zenghi said, "Allah, what dogs are these Christians, who betray and cut one another's throats for the promise of gold or land!"

"Is it well to trust such a man?" queried Ousama. "If he will betray his kind, he will surely betray you if he may."

"May I eat pork if I trust him," retorted Zenghi, moving a chessman with a jeweled finger. "As I move this pawn I will move the dog-emperor of the Greeks. With his aid I will crack the kings of Outremer like nutshells. I have promised him their seaports, and he will keep his promises until he thinks his prizes are in his hands. Ha! Not towns but the sword-edge I will give him. What we take together shall be mine, nor will that suffice me. By Allah, not Mesopotamia, nor Syria, nor all Asia Minor is enough! I will cross the Hellespont! I will ride my stallion through the palaces on the Golden Horn! Frankistan herself shall tremble before me!"

The impact of his voice was like that of a harsh-throated trumpet, almost stunning the hearers with its dynamic intensity. His eyes blazed, his fingers knotted like iron on the chessboard.

"You are old, Zenghi," warned the cautious Arab. "You have done much. Is there no limit to your ambitions?"

"Aye!" laughed the Turk. "The horn of the moon and the points of the stars! Old? Eleven years older than thyself, and younger in spirit than thou wert ever. My thews are steel, my heart is fire, my wits keener even than on the day

I broke ibn Sadaka beside the Nile and set my feet on the shining stairs of glory! Peace, here comes the Frank."

A small boy of about eight years of age, sitting cross-legged on a cushion near the edge of the dais whereon lay Zenghi's divan, had been staring up in rapt adoration. His fine brown eyes sparkled as Zenghi spoke of his ambition, and his small frame quivered with excitement, as if his soul had taken fire from the Turk's wild words. Now he looked at the entrance of the pavilion with the others, as the memluks entered with the visitor between them, his scabbard empty. They had taken his weapons outside the royal tent.

The memluks fell back and ranged themselves on either side of the dais, leaving the Frank in an open space before their master. Zenghi's keen eyes swept over the tall form in its glittering gold-worked mail, took in the clean-shaven face with its cold eyes, and rested on the Koran-inscribed ring on the man's finger.

"My master, the emperor of Byzantium," said the Frank in Turki, "sends thee greeting, oh Zenghi, Lion of Islam."

As he spoke he took in the details of the impressive figure, clad in steel, silk and gold, before him; the strong dark face, the powerful frame which, despite the years, betokened steel-spring muscles and unquenchable vitality; above all the Atabeg's eyes, gleaming with unperishable youth and innate fierceness.

"And what said thy master, oh Wulfgar?" asked the Turk.

"He sends thee this letter," answered the Frank, drawing forth a packet and proffering it to Yaruktash, who in turn, and on his knees, delivered it to Zenghi. The Atabeg perused the parchment, signed in the Emperor's unmistakable hand and sealed with the royal Byzantine seal. Zenghi never dealt with underlings, but always with the highest power of friends or foes.

"The seals have been broken," said the Turk, fixing his piercing eyes on the inscrutable countenance of the Frank. "Thou hast read?"

"Aye. I was pursued by men of the prince of Antioch, and fearing lest I be seized and searched, I opened the missive and read it, so that if I were forced to destroy it lest it fall into enemy hands, I could repeat the message to thee by word of mouth."

"Let me hear, then, if thy memory be equal to thy discretion," commanded the Atabeg.

"As thou wilt. My master says to thee, 'Concerning that which hath passed between us, I must have better proof of thy good faith. Wherefore do thou send me by this messenger, who, though unknown to thee, is a man to be trusted, full details of thy desires and good proof of the aid thou hast promised us in the proposed movement against Antioch. Before I put to sea I must know that thou art ready to move by land, and there must be binding oaths between us.' And the missive is signed with the emperor's own hand."

The Turk nodded; a mirthful devil danced in his blue eyes.

"They are his very words. Blessed is the monarch who boasts such a vassal. Sit ye upon that heap of cushions; meat and drink shall be brought to you."

Calling Yaruktash, Zenghi whispered in his ear. The eunuch started, stared, and then salaamed and hastened from the pavilion. Slaves brought food and the forbidden wine in golden vessels, and the Frank broke his fast with unfeigned relish. Zenghi watched him inscrutably and the glittering memluks stood like statues of burnished steel.

"You came first to Edessa?" asked the Atabeg.

"Nay. When I left my ship at Antioch I set forth for Edessa, but I had scarce crossed the border when a band of wandering Arabs, recognizing your ring, told me you were on the march for Rakka, thence to Mosul. So I turned aside and rode to cut your line of march, and my way being made clear for me by virtue of the ring which all your subjects know, I was at last met by the chief Il-Ghazi who escorted me thither."

Zenghi nodded his leonine head slowly.

"Mosul calls me. I go back to my capital to gather my hawks, to brace my lines. When I return I will sweep the Franks into the sea with the aid of--thy master.

"But I forget the courtesy due a guest. This is the prince Ousama of Sheyzar, and this child is the son of my friend Nejm-ed-din, who saved my army and my life when I fled from Karaja the Cup-bearer--one of the few foes who ever saw my back. His father dwells at Baalbekk, which I gave him to rule, but I have taken Yusef with me to look on Mosul. Verily, he is more to me than my own sons. I have named him Salah-ed-din, and he shall be a thorn in the flesh of Christendom."

At this instant Yaruktash entered and whispered in Zenghi's ear, and the Atabeg nodded.

As the eunuch withdrew, Zenghi turned to the Frank. The Turk's manner had changed subtly. His lids drooped over his glittering eyes and a faint hint of mockery curled his bearded lips.

"I would show you one whose countenance you know of old," said he.

The Frank looked up in surprise.

"Have I a friend in the hosts of Mosul?"

"You shall see!" Zenghi clapped his hands, and Yaruktash, appearing at the door of the pavilion grasping a slender white wrist, dragged the owner into view and cast her from him so that she fell to the carpet almost at the Frank's feet. With a terrible cry he started up, his face deathly.

"Ellen! My God! Alive!"

"Miles!" she echoed his cry, struggling to her knees. In a mist of stupefaction he saw her white arms outstretched, her pale face framed in the golden hair which fell over the white shoulders the scanty harim garb left bare. Forgetting all else he fell to his knees beside her, gathering her into his arms.

"Ellen! Ellen de Tremont! I had scoured the world for you and hacked a path through the legions of Hell itself--but they said you were dead. Musa, before he died at my feet, swore he saw you lying in your blood among the corpses of your servants in your courtyard."

"Would God it had been so!" she sobbed, her golden head against his steel-clad breast. "But when they cut down my servants I fell among the bodies in a swoon, and their blood stained my garments; so men thought me dead. It was Zenghi himself who found me alive, and took me--" She hid her face in her hands.

"And so, Sir Miles du Courcey," broke in the sardonic voice of the Turk, "you have found a friend among the Mosuli! Fool! My senses are keener than a whetted sword. Think you I did not know you, despite your clean-shaven face? I saw you too often on the ramparts of Edessa, hewing down my memluks. I knew you as soon as you entered. What have you done with the real messenger?"

Grimly Miles disengaged himself from the girl's clinging arms and rose, facing the Atabeg. Zenghi likewise rose, quick and lithe as a great panther, and drew his scimitar, while from all sides the heron-feathered memluks began to edge in silently. Miles' hand fell away from his empty scabbard and his eyes rested for an instant on something close to his feet--a curved knife, used for carving fruit, and lying there forgotten, half-hidden under a cushion.

"Wulfgar Edric's son lies dead among the trees on the Antioch road," said Miles grimly. "I shaved off my beard and took his armor and the ring the dog bore."

"The better to spy on me," quoth Zenghi.

"Aye." There was no fear in Miles du Courcey. "I wished to learn the details of the plot you hatched with John Comnene, and to obtain proofs of his treachery and your ambitions to show to the lords of Outremer."

"I deduced as much," smiled Zenghi. "I knew you, as I said. But I wished you to betray yourself fully; hence the girl, who has spoken your name with weeping many times in the years of her captivity."

"It was an unworthy gesture and one in keeping with your character," said Miles somberly. "Yet I thank you for allowing me to see her once more, and to know that she is alive whom I thought long dead."

"I have done her great honor," answered Zenghi laughing. "She has been in my harim for two years."

Miles' grim eyes only grew more somber, but the great veins swelled almost to bursting along his temples. At his feet the girl covered her face with her white hands and wept silently. The boy on the cushion looked about uncertainly, not understanding. Ousama's fine eyes were touched with pity. But Zenghi grinned broadly. Such scenes were like wine to the Turk, shaking inwardly with the gargantuan laughter of his breed.

"You shall bless me for my bounty, Sir Miles," said Zenghi. "For my kingly generosity you shall give praise. Lo, the girl is yours! When I tear you between four wild horses tomorrow, she shall accompany you to Hell on a pointed stake--ha!"

Like a striking cobra Miles du Courcey had moved. Snatching the knife from beneath the cushion he leaped-- not at the guarded Atabeg on the divan, but at the child on the edge of the dais. Before any could stop him, he caught up the boy Saladin with one hand, and with the other pressed the curved edge to his throat.

"Back, dogs!" His voice cracked with mad triumph. "Back, or I send this heathen spawn to Hell!"

Zenghi, his face livid, yelled a frenzied order, and the memluks fell back. Then while the Atabeg stood trembling and uncertain, at a loss for the first and only time of his whole wild career, du Courcey backed toward the door, holding his captive, who neither cried out nor struggled. The contemplative brown eyes showed no fear, only a fatalistic resignation of a philosophy beyond the owner's years.

"To me, Ellen!" snapped the Norman, his somber despair changed to dynamic action. "Out of the door behind me--back dogs, I say!"

Out of the pavilion he backed, and the memluks who ran up, sword in hand, stopped short as they saw the imminent peril of their lord's favorite. Du Courcey knew that the success of his action depended on speed. The surprize and boldness of his move had taken Zenghi off guard, that was all. A group of horses stood near by, saddled and bridled, always ready for the Atabeg's whim, and du Courcey reached them with a single long stride, the grooms falling back from his threat.

"Into a saddle, Ellen!" he snapped, and the girl, who had followed him like one in a daze, reacting mechanically to his orders, swung herself up on the nearest mount. Quickly he followed suit and cut the tethers that held their mounts. A bellow from inside the tent told him Zenghi's momentarily scattered wits were working again, and he dropped the child unhurt into the sand. His usefulness was past, as a hostage. Zenghi, taken by surprize, had instinctively followed the promptings of his unusual affection for the child, but Miles knew that with his ruthless reason dominating him again, the Atabeg would not allow even that affection to stand in the way of their recapture.

The Norman wheeled away, drawing Ellen's steed with him, trying to shield her with his own body from the arrows which were already whistling about them. Shoulder to shoulder they raced across the wide open space in front of the royal pavilion, burst through a ring of fires, floundered for an instant among tent-pegs, cords and scurrying yelling figures, then struck the open desert flying and heard the clamor die out behind them.

It was dark, clouds flying across the sky and drowning the stars. With the clatter of hoofs behind them, Miles reined aside from the road that led westward, and turned into the trackless desert. Behind them the hoof-beats faded westward. The pursuers had taken the old caravan road, supposing the fugitives to be ahead of them.

"What now, Miles?" Ellen was riding alongside, and clinging to his iron-sheathed arm as if she feared he might fade suddenly from her sight.

"If we ride straight for the border they will have us before dawn," he answered. "But I know this land as well as they--I have ridden all over it of old in foray and war with the counts of Edessa; so I know that Jabar Kal'at lies within our reach to the southwest. The commander of Jabar is a nephew of Muin-ed-din Anar, who is the real ruler of Damascus, and who, as perhaps you know, has made a pact with the Christians against Zenghi, his old rival. If we can reach Jabar, the commander will give us shelter and food, and fresh horses and an escort to the border."

The girl bowed her head in acquiescence. She was still like one dazed. The light of hope burned too feebly in her soul to sting her with new pangs. Perhaps in her captivity she had absorbed some of the fatalism of her masters. Miles looked at her, drooping in the saddle, humble and silent, and thought of the picture he retained of a saucy, laughing beauty, vibrant with vitality and mirth. And he cursed Zenghi and his works with sick fury. So through the night they rode, the broken woman and the embittered man, handiworks of the Lion who dealt in swords and souls and human hearts, and whose victims, living and dead, filled the land like a blight of sorrow, agony and despair.

All night they pressed forward as fast as they dared, listening for sounds that would tell them the pursuers had found their trail, and in the dawn, which lit the helmets of swift-following horsemen, they saw the towers of Jabar rising above the mirroring waters of the Euphrates. It was a strong keep, guarded with a moat that encircled it, connecting with the river at either end. At their hail the commander of the castle appeared on the wall, and a few words sufficed to cause the drawbridge to be lowered. It was not a moment too soon. As they clattered across the bridge, the drum of hoofs was in their ears, and as they passed through the gates, arrows fell in a shower about them.

The leader of the pursuers reined his rearing steed and called arrogantly to the commander on the tower. "Oh man, give up these fugitives, lest thy blood quench the embers of thy keep!"

"Am I then a dog that you speak to me thus?" queried the Seljuk, clutching his beard in passion. "Begone, or my archers will feather thy carcass with fifty shafts."

For answer the memluk laughed jeeringly and pointed to the desert. The commander paled. Far away the sun glinted on a moving ocean of steel. His practiced eye told him that a whole army was on the march.

"Zenghi has turned from his march to hunt down a pair of fleeing jackals," called the memluk mockingly. "Great honor he has done them, marching hard on their spoor all night. Send them out, oh fool, and my master will ride on in peace."

"Let it be as Allah wills," said the Seljuk, recovering his poise. "But the friends of my uncle have thrown themselves into my hands, and may shame rest on me and mine if I give them to the butcher."

Nor did he alter his resolution when Zenghi himself, his face dark with passion as the cloak that flowed from his steel-clad shoulders, sat his stallion beneath the towers and called: "Oh man, by receiving mine enemy thou hast forfeited thy castle and thy life. Yet I will be merciful. Send out those who fled and I will allow thee to march out unharmed with thy women and retainers. Persist in this madness and I will burn thee like a rat in thy castle."

"Let it be as Allah wills," repeated the Seljuk philosophically, and in an undertone spoke quietly to a crouching archer, "Drive quickly a shaft through yon dog."

The arrow glanced harmlessly from Zenghils breastplate and the Atabeg galloped out of range with a shout of mocking laughter. Now began the siege of Jabar Kal'at, unsung and unglorified, yet in the course of which the dice of Fate were cast.

Zenghi's riders laid waste the surrounding countryside and drew a cordon about the castle through which no courier could steal to ride for aid. While the emir of Damascus and the lords of Outremer remained in ignorance of what was taking place beyond the Euphrates, their ally waged his unequal battle.

By nightfall the wagons and siege engines came up, and Zenghi set to his task with the skill of long practice. The Turkish sappers dammed up the moat at the upper end, despite the arrows of the defenders, and filled up the drained ditch with earth and stone. Under cover of darkness they sank mines beneath the towers. Zenghi's ballistas creaked and crashed and huge rocks knocked men off the walls like tenpins or smashed through the roof of the towers. His rams gnawed and pounded at the walls, his archers plied the turrets with their arrows everlastingly, and on scaling-ladders and storming-towers his memluks moved unceasingly to the onset. Food waned in the castle's larders; the heaps of dead grew larger, the rooms became full of wounded men, groaning and writhing.

But the Seljuk commander did not falter on the path his feet had taken. He knew that he could not now buy safety from Zenghi, even by giving up his guests; to his credit, he never even considered giving them up. Du Courcey knew this, and though no word of the matter was spoken between them, the commander had evidence of the Norman's fierce gratitude. Miles showed his appreciation in actions, not words--in the fighting on the walls, in the slaughter in the gates, in the long night-watches on the towers; with whirring sword-strokes that clove bucklers and peaked helmets, that cleft spines and severed necks and limbs and shattered skulls; by the casting down of scaling-ladders when the clinging Turks howled as they crashed to their death, and their comrades cried out at the terrible strength in the Frank's naked hands. But the rams crunched, the arrows sang, the steel tides surged on again and again, and the haggard defenders dropped one by one until only a skeleton force held the crumbling walls of Jabar Kal'at.

CHAPTER 5

In his pavilion little more than a bowshot from the beleaguered walls, Zenghi played chess with Ousama. The madness of the day had given way to the brooding silence of night, broken only by the distant cries of wounded men in delirium.

"Men are my pawns, friend," said the Atabeg. "I turn adversity into triumph. I had long sought an excuse to attack Jabar Kal'at, which will make a strong outpost against the Franks once I have taken it and repaired the dents I have made, and filled it with my memluks. I knew my captives would ride hither; that is why I broke camp and took up the march before my scouts found their tracks. It was their logical refuge. I will have the castle and the Franks, which last is most vital. Were the Caphars to learn now of my intrigue with the emperor, my plans might well come to naught. But they will not know until I strike. Du Courcey will never bear news to them. If he does not fall with the castle, I will tear him between wild horses as I promised, and the infidel girl shall watch, sitting on a pointed stake."

"Is there no mercy in your soul, Zenghi?" protested the Arab.

"Has life shown mercy to me save what I wrung forth by the sword?" exclaimed Zenghi, his eyes blazing in a momentary upheaval of his passionate spirit. "A man must smite or be smitten--slay or be slain. Men are wolves, and I am but the strongest wolf of the pack. Because they fear me, men crawl and kiss my sandals. Fear is the only emotion by which they may be touched."

"You are a pagan at heart, Zenghi," sighed Ousama.

"It may be," answered the Turk with a shrug of his shoulders. "Had I been born beyond the Oxus and bowed to yellow Erlik as did my grandsire, I had been no less Zenghi the Lion. I have spilled rivers of gore for the glory of Allah, but I have never asked mercy or favor of Him. What care the gods if a man lives or dies? Let me live deep, let me know the sting of wine in my palate, the wind in my face, the glitter of royal pageantry, the bright madness of slaughter--let me burn and sting and tingle with the madness of life and living, and I quest not whether Muhammad's paradise, or Erlik's frozen hell, or the blackness of empty-oblivion lies beyond."

As if to give point to his words, he poured himself a goblet of wine and looked interrogatively at Ousama. The Arab, who had shuddered at Zenghi's blasphemous words, drew back in pious horror. The Atabeg emptied the goblet, smacking his lips loudly in relish, Tatar-fashion.

"I think Jabar Kal'at will fall tomorrow," he said. "Who has stood against me? Count them, Ousama--there was ibn Sadaka, and the Caliph, and the Seljuk Timurtash, and the sultan Dawud, and the king of Jerusalem, and the count of Edessa. Man after man, city after city, army after army, I broke them and brushed them from my path."

"You have waded through a sea of blood," said Ousama. "You have filled the slave-markets with Frankish girls, and the deserts with the bones of Frankish warriors. Nor have you spared your rivals among the Moslems."

"They stood in the way of my destiny," laughed the Turk, "and that destiny is to be sultan of Asia! As I will be. I have welded the swords of Irak, el Jezira, Syria and Roum, into a single blade. Now with the aid of the Greeks, all Hell can not save the Nazarenes. Slaughter? Men have seen naught; wait until I ride into Antioch and Jerusalem, sword in hand!"

"Your heart is steel," said the Arab. "Yet I have seen one touch of tenderness in you--your affection for Nejm-ed-din's son, Yusef. Is there a like touch of repentance in you? Of all your deeds, is there none you regret?"

Zenghi played with a pawn in silence, and his face darkened.

"Aye," he said slowly. "It was long ago, when I broke ibn Sadaka beside the lower reaches of this very river. He had a son, Achmet, a girl-faced boy. I beat him to death with my riding-scourge. It is the one deed I could wish undone. Sometimes I dream of it."

Then with an abrupt "Enough!" he thrust aside the board, scattering the chessmen. "I would sleep," said he, and throwing himself on his cushion-heaped divan, he was instantly locked in slumber. Ousama went quietly from the tent, passing between the four giant memluks in gilded mail who stood with wide-tipped scimitars at the pavilion door.

In the castle of Jabar, the Seljuk commander held counsel with Sir Miles du Courcey. "My brother, for us the end of the road has come. The walls are crumbling, the towers leaning to their fall. Shall we not fire the castle, cut the throats of our women and children, and go forth to die like men in the dawn?"

Sir Miles shook his head. "Let us hold the walls for one more day. In a dream I saw the banners of Damascus and of Antioch marching to our aid."

He lied in a desperate attempt to bolster up the fatalistic Seljuk. Each followed the instinct of his kind, and Miles was to cling with teeth and nails to the last vestige of life until the bitter end. The Seljuk bowed his head.

"If Allah wills, we will hold the walls for another day."

Miles thought of Ellen, into whose manner something of the old vibrant spirit was beginning to steal faintly again, and in the blackness of his despair no light gleamed from earth or heaven. The finding of her had stung to life a heart long frozen; now in death he must lose her again. With the taste of bitter ashes in his mouth he bent his shoulders anew to the burden of life.

In his tent Zenghi moved restlessly. Alert as a panther, even in sleep, his instinct told him that someone was moving stealthily near him. He woke and sat up glaring. The fat eunuch Yaruktash halted suddenly, the wine jug halfway to his lips. He had thought Zenghi lay helplessly drunk when he stole into the tent to filch the liquor he loved. Zenghi snarled like a wolf, his familiar devil rising in his brain.

"Dog! Am I a fat merchant that you steal into my tent to guzzle my wine? Begone! Tomorrow I will see to you!"

Cold sweat beaded Yaruktash's sleek hide as he fled from the royal pavilion. His fat flesh quivered with agonized anticipation of the sharp stake which would undoubtedly be his portion. In a day of cruel masters, Zenghi's name was a byword of horror among slaves and servitors.

One of the memluks outside the tent caught Yaruktash's arm and growled, "Why flee you, gelding?"

A great flare of light rose in the eunuch's brain, so that he gasped at its grandeur and audacity. Why remain here to be impaled, when the whole desert was open before him, and here were men who would protect him in his flight?

"Our lord discovered me drinking his wine," he gasped. "He threatens me with torture and death."

The memluks laughed appreciatively, their crude humor touched by the eunuch's fright. Then they started convulsively as Yaruktash added, "You too are doomed. I heard him curse you for not keeping better watch, and allowing his slaves to steal his wine."

The fact that they had never been told to bar the eunuch from the royal pavilion meant nothing to the memluks, their wits frozen with sudden fear. They stood dumbly, incapable of coherent thought, their minds like empty jugs ready to be filled with the eunuch's guile. A few whispered words and they slunk away like shadows on Yaruktash's heels, leaving the pavilion unguarded.

The night waned. Midnight hovered and was gone. The moon sank below the desert hills in a welter of blood. From dreams of imperial pageantry Zenghi again awoke, to stare bewilderedly about the dim-lit pavilion. Without, all was silence that seemed suddenly tense and sinister. The prince lay in the midst of ten thousand armed men; yet he felt suddenly apart and alone, as if he were the last man left alive on a dead world. Then he saw that he was not alone. Looking somberly down on him stood a strange and alien figure. It was a man, whose rags did not hide his gaunt limbs, at which Zenghi stared appalled. They were gnarled like the twisted branches of ancient oaks, knotted with masses of muscle and thews, each of which stood out distinct, like iron cables. There was no soft flesh to lend symmetry or to mask the raw savagery of sheer power. Only years of incredible labor could have produced this terrible monument of muscular overdevelopment. White hair hung about the great shoulders, a white beard fell upon the mighty breast. His terrible arms were folded, and he stood motionless as a statue looking down upon the stupefied Turk. His features were gaunt and deep-lined, as if cut by some mad artist's chisel from bitter, frozen rock.

"Avaunt!" gasped Zenghi, momentarily a pagan of the steppes. "Spirit of evil--ghost of the desert--demon of the hills--I fear you not!"

"Well may you speak of ghosts, Turk!" The deep hollow voice woke dim memories in Zenghi's brain. "I am the ghost of a man dead twenty years, come up from darkness deeper than the darkness of Hell. Have you forgotten my promise, Prince Zenghi?"

"Who are you?" demanded the Turk.

"I am John Norwald."

"The Frank who rode with ibn Sadaka? Impossible!" ejaculated the Atabeg. "Twenty-three years ago I doomed him to the rower's bench. What galley-slave could live so long?"

"I lived," retorted the other. "Where others died like flies, I lived. The lash that scarred my back in a thousand overlying patterns could not kill me, nor starvation, nor storm, nor pestilence, nor battle. The years have been long, Zenghi esh Shami, and the darkness deep and full of mocking voices and haunting faces. Look at my hair,

47

Zenghi--white as hoarfrost, though I am eight years younger than yourself. Look at these monstrous talons that were hands, these knotted limbs--they have driven the weighted oars for many a thousand leagues through storm and calm. Yet I lived, Zenghi, even when my flesh cried out to end the long agony. When I fainted on the oar, it was not ripping lash that roused me to life anew, but the hate that would not let me die. That hate has kept the soul in my tortured body for twenty-three years, dog of Tiberias. In the galleys I lost my youth, my hope, my manhood, my soul, my faith and my God. But my hate burned on, a flame that nothing could quench.

"Twenty years at the oars, Zenghi! Three years ago the galley in which I then toiled crashed on the reefs off the coast of India. All died but me, who, knowing my hour had come, burst my chains with the strength and madness of a giant, and gained the shore. My feet are yet unsteady from the shackles and the galley-bench, Zenghi, though my arms are strong beyond the belief of man. I have been on the road from India for three years. But the road ends here."

For the first time in his life Zenghi knew fear that froze his tongue to his palate and turned the marrow in his bones to ice.

"Ho, guards!" he roared. "To me, dogs!"

"Call louder, Zenghi!" said Norwald in his hollow resounding voice. "They hear thee not. Through thy sleeping host I passed like the Angel of Death, and none saw me. Thy tent stood unguarded. Lo, mine enemy, thou art delivered into my hand, and thine hour has come!"

With the ferocity of desperation Zenghi leaped from his cushions, whipping out a dagger, but like a great gaunt tiger the Englishman was upon him, crushing him back on the divan. The Turk struck blindly, felt the blade sink deep into the other's side; then as he wrenched the weapon free to strike again, he felt an iron grip on his wrist, and the Frank's right hand locked on his throat, choking his cry.

As he felt the inhuman strength of his attacker, blind panic swept the Atabeg. The fingers on his wrist did not feel like human bone and flesh and sinew. They were like the steel jaws of a vise that crushed through flesh and muscle. Over the inexorable fingers that sank into his bull-throat, blood trickled from skin torn like rotten cloth. Mad with the torture of strangulation, Zenghi tore at the wrist with his free hand, but he might have been wrenching at a steel bar welded to his throat. The massed muscles of Norwald's left arm knotted with effort, and with a sickening snap Zenghi's wrist bones gave way. The dagger fell from his nerveless hand, and instantly Norwald caught it up and sank the point into the Atabeg's breast.

The Turk released the arm that prisoned his throat, and caught the knife-wrist, but all his desperate strength could not stay the inexorable thrust. Slowly, slowly, Norwald drove home the keen point, while the Turk writhed in soundless agony. Approaching through the mists which veiled his glazing sight, Zenghi saw a face, raw, torn and bleeding. And then the dagger-point found his heart and visions and life ended together.

Ousama, unable to sleep, approached the Atabeg's tent, wondering at the absence of the guardsmen. He stopped short, an uncanny fear prickling the short hairs at the back of his neck, as a form came from the pavilion. He made out a tall white-bearded man, clad in rags. The Arab stretched forth a hand timidly, but dared not touch the apparition. He saw that the figure's hand was pressed against its left side, and blood oozed darkly from between the fingers.

"Where go you, old man?" stammered the Arab, involuntarily stepping back as the white-bearded stranger fixed weird blazing eyes upon him.

"I go back to the void which gave me birth," answered the figure in a deep ghostly voice, and as the Arab stared in bewilderment, the stranger passed on with slow, certain, unwavering steps, to vanish in the darkness.

Ousama ran into Zenghi's tent--to halt aghast at sight of the Atabeg's body lying stark among the torn silks and bloodstained cushions of the royal divan.

"Alas for kingly ambitions and high visions!" exclaimed the Arab. "Death is a black horse that may halt in the night by any tent, and life is more unstable than the foam on the sea! Woe for Islam, for her keenest sword is broken! Now may Christendom rejoice, for the Lion that roared against her lies lifeless!"

Like wildfire ran through the camp the word of the Atabeg's death, and like chaff blown on the winds his followers scattered, looting the camp as they fled. The power that had welded them together was broken, and it was every man for himself, and the plunder to the strong.

The haggard defenders on the walls, lifting their notched stumps of blades for the last death-grapple, gaped as they saw the confusion in the camp, the running to and fro, the brawling, the looting and shouting, and at last the scattering over the plain of emirs and retainers alike. These hawks lived by the sword, and they had no time for the dead, however regal. They turned their steeds aside to seek a new lord, in a race for the strongest.

Stunned by the miracle, not yet understanding the cast of Fate that had saved Jabar Kal'at and Outremer, Miles du Courcey stood with Ellen and their Seljuk friend, staring down on a silent and abandoned camp, where the torn deserted tent flapped idly in the morning breeze above the bloodstained body that had been the Lion of Tiberias.